Bamboo, Velvet and Beak
are sitting on their log in
the middle of the rainforest -
just as they always do.

'What did you two have for breakfast?' asks Bamboo.

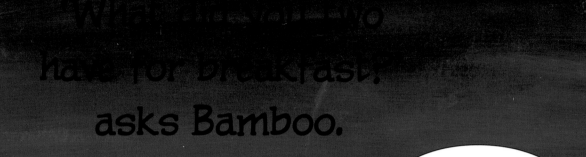

Grass

says Velvet. 'Followed by a moss salad with lemon dressing.'

Bamboo, Velvet and Beak

The Lunch

Felicia Law

Illustrated by Nicola Evans

allegra

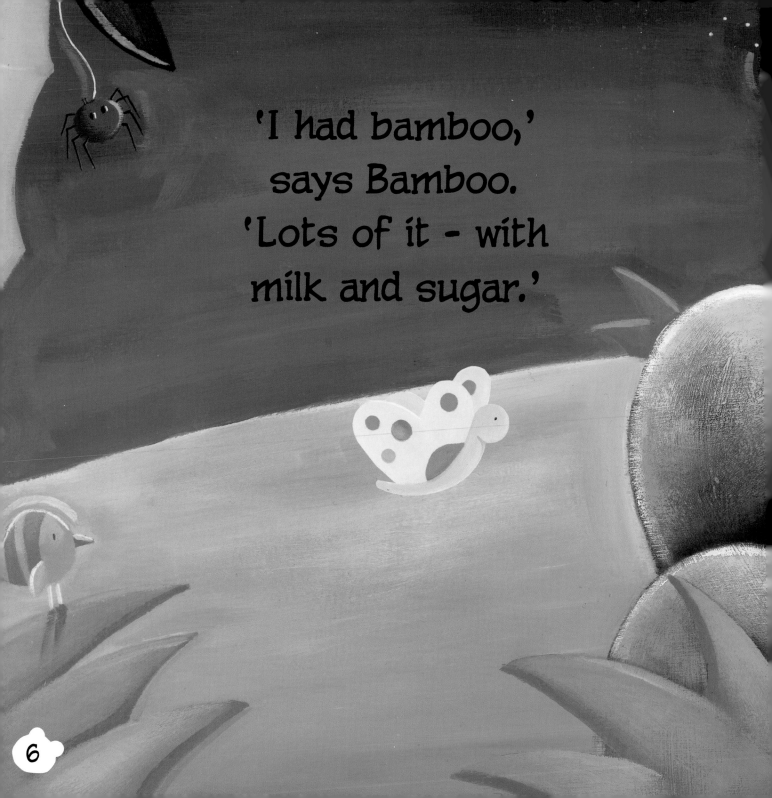

'I had bamboo,'
says Bamboo.
'Lots of it - with
milk and sugar.'

6

'What did you have for lunch?' asks Bamboo.

'Ladybird on toast and slug sauce,' says Beak.

8

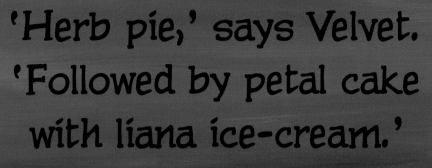

'Herb pie,' says Velvet.
'Followed by petal cake
with liana ice-cream.'

9

'I had bamboo. Lots of it – with ketchup,' says Bamboo.

10

'...shrooms, followed
by banana leaf
crumble with
fern topping,'
says Velvet.

'Soft-shell snails,'
says Beak.

You have to eat bamboo
three times a day?
That's unbelievable!'
say Velvet and Beak.

15

'My mum says bamboo is good for me,' says Bamboo.

'She says I have to eat it
'cos it'll make me big and strong.'

"I'd hate a mum like that,"
says Velvet, shaking her head.

21

'And anyway, my mum says
you can never have enough
of a good thing.'

The stories in the 'Bamboo, Velvet and Beak' series
find the three animals sitting together, observing
the rainforest and the events that come
and go around them.

Other titles in the series:
The Daddy-long-legs; The Rainbow;
The Creeper; The Walk;
The Tree; The Feathers; The Flower;
The Furry Caterpillar; The Bird.

ISBN 978-1-906292-01-0
Printed in China